ARMAGEDDON

Armageddon
Copyright © 2023 by Clarence Causby

Published in the United States of America
ISBN   Paperback: 978-1-959761-82-2
ISBN   eBook: 978-1-959761-83-9

All rights reserved. No part of this publication may be reproduced, stored in a retrieval system or transmitted in any way by any means, electronic, mechanical, photocopy, recording or otherwise without the prior permission of the author except as provided by USA copyright law.

The opinions expressed by the author are not necessarily those of ReadersMagnet, LLC.

ReadersMagnet, LLC
10620 Treena Street, Suite 230 | San Diego, California, 92131 USA
1.619. 354. 2643 | www.readersmagnet.com

Book design copyright © 2023 by ReadersMagnet, LLC. All rights reserved.

Cover design by Arnaldo Rosado
Interior design by Ched Celiz

ARMAGEDDON

CLARENCE CAUSBY

ReadersMagnet, LLC

WARNING!!!!!!!!!!!!!!!!!

This book is just what it is, a book. I do not know how Armageddon will play out, and hope not to be here for Armageddon. This is just my interpretation. Do not come for me saying this is not how this or that will happen. If you're here for when Armageddon happens, then you will know first-hand how it will happen. Like I said, this is just my interpretation. Do not come for me at all!!!!!

CHAPTER 1

It was a hot summer day in the middle of July. It was one hundred and fourteen degrees in Oklahoma, on a Sunday morning. Driving down the road is a red convertible with three friends in it.

The driver is twenty-five years old, he is six foot two, with short blonde hair and fair skin, his name is Jonathan. His friend in the passenger seat is named Bobby, he is five foot four, Spanish and light-skinned, he is twenty-five years old as well. Their friend in the back is named Alexander, but his friends call him Alex. He is five foot seven, black and light-skinned. He is twenty-four years old.

"Hey Alex, why are we going to church again? I'd rather be out trying to go on a date, or at least watching a movie and playing games," said Bobby.

Jonathan laughed. "He's not wrong Alex, we could be at the beach or doing something better or fun, then going to a church," said Jonathan.

"Yeah, yeah, I know, but on the anniversary of my parents' death, I had made them a promise to go to church. So today is the day," replied Alex.

The three friends arrived at the church. "This is a nice sized church," observed Jonathan. They got out of the car and walked inside the church.

The church members greeted the three friends. They sat down, after a few songs by the choir, the pastor proceeded to the pulpit, everyone in the church stood up. The pastor said a prayer, greeted the members of the church and told the congregation to have a seat. The congregation sat down.

"God bless all of you on this fine day," said the pastor. "For the visitors that came here today, I greet you welcome, in the name of the Lord. I am Apostle Janine Davenport. Today, I want to show everyone something that was on the news, in case some of you missed it." Apostle Davenport pulled up a news broadcast on the huge screen.

"Hello everyone, thank you for tuning in to the eleven o'clock breaking news. This just in ladies and gentleman, Pastor Xavier Townsend and his wife Sarah and their three kids have gone missing. No one has any idea where he and his family are. His brothers and sisters have all gone missing as well," opened the reporter. "Seems like numerous people have been missing as well," the reporter continued.

"Ladies and gentlemen, we seem to be having an issue at the newsroom well." Brandon the cameraman spun around to show the remaining few members of the otherwise extensive news crew. "We have some footage of some of the disappearing people." Clips of disappearing people from all over the world flashed across the screen.

"We can cut it off," said Apostle Davenport. "Church, I can only think of one thing that this could be. I'm not saying I'm right or wrong, but I'm telling you what I think it may be. This seems to be the time of the rapture. I can't explain why people are just disappearing." Apostle Davenport started to preach for an hour. "I hear the Lord saying that I must call an altar call; right now if there is anyone that wants to be saved, raise your hand and say this prayer and mean it with all sincerity."

After the altar call, Apostle Davenport proceeded to give the benediction, "Everyone close your eyes and lift your hands."

A long, odd silence followed. Alex opened his eyes, looked around and saw only five people, plus his friends. Alex nudged Jonathan. Jonathan opened his eyes and saw the five people that were there plus Alex and Bobby. He nudged Bobby, Bobby opened his eyes and saw what everyone else saw.

"What is going on?" said Bobby. "Is this a joke? Do they do this at all churches or just this one? Excuse me," Bobby turned to the five people in the other seats, "are you regular members here or visitors?"

"We're members," said a woman from the front seat.

"Does this usually happen or is this a joke?"

"No, we've never had this happen ever! It must be like the Apostle said, this has to be the time of the rapture.",

"Yeah, ok, sure have fun with that," said Jonathan. "Let's go boys, time to have some fun." The three friends got up and walked out of the church. "Well now that that's done, let's go and have some fun."

The three friends hopped in the car. "Where to now gentlemen?" asked Bobby.

"Let's head to San Francisco."

As the three friends drove off towards California, Alex asked, "What do you think that was about, at the church?"

"Who knows, it could have been a joke," Bobby replied.

"How could all those people have left in that short amount of time?" asked Alex.

"Who knows," said Jonathan. "Who cares? We're going and having some fun. It could have all been staged."

"That fast though?" wondered Bobby.

"Does it really matter? Let's forget about it and enjoy ourselves on this great trip we're taking," Jonathon replied.

As the friends continued on their drive, they saw cars on the other side of the highway not moving at all.

"What is going on over there?" asked Alex as he was driving.

"LOOK OUT!!!" Jonathan yelled as he tried to grab the steering wheel. Alex quickly slammed the brakes. "Sorry about that guys," Alex said.

"What is going on here?" asked Jonathan. There were lots of cars that had crashed or were just not moving at all. Bobby and Jonathan jumped out of the car, and went to look at the other cars.

"Hey Alex come check this out," said Bobby.

Alex got out, the cars were empty. "Is this like some kind of zombie apocalypse?"

I don't know about a zombie apocalypse but the actual apocalypse may be happening. Let's get back in the car and get out of here," Bobby suggested.

The three friends got back into the car and drove onto the grass to get around the crash. They drove for five miles until they finally cleared it. There was barely anyone on the road.

They stopped to get some gas, pick up some snacks and stretch their legs before they switched drivers. After a day and hours of driving, seeing more abandoned and crashed cars along the way, they finally reached California. "So glad we got to California," said Alex. "Now we just need to make our way to San Francisco. Let's get something to eat first."

"Yeah we've been riding for a while, let's get a burger or tacos, or pizza or something," Bobby said. They walked into a restaurant where they saw bags and bags of food on the counter. They asked an employee what happened to the people that ordered their food. The employee said that as he turned to get their food, they just disappeared. The food had been sitting there for about ten minutes. "You can have it if you want," he told them. "Thanks so much," Jonathan replied. The friends grabbed the food.

They heard a noise. The employee yelled. "Hey are you ok back there?" asked Alex. The employee came back and said he literally saw one of his coworkers disappear in front of his eyes. A few of his other remaining coworkers came back to the front where the friends were and told them to enjoy the food. "We're leaving, only five of us are here and people have disappeared, including our manager, supervisor and district manager. The food is already paid for." The employees left the building.

Alex, Bobby and Jonathan heard a noise. They turned around and saw the employee that was helping them open the registers and take all the cash. "I'm giving myself a raise, take care and don't say a word about this." He left with the money in garbage bags and a burrito in his mouth.

Bobby, Jonathan and Alex went back to the car. They continued on their trip. The sun was setting as they got closer to San Francisco. They went across the Golden Gate Bridge. They checked into a hotel, went into their rooms, and a few hours later decided to take a tour of the city. They saw empty buildings and empty cars for miles, there were a few people every once in a while. They saw people looking around, asking what was going on. They saw a lady praying and asking for forgiveness. As they were walking, they saw the woman disappear in front of their eyes. They fell back in shock.

"What…what was that just now?" asked Jonathan.

"You saw the same thing we did," answered Bobby.

"This is crazy, this is like from some kind of movie," replied Alex. "You know I think that Pastor, whatever her name was, was right. This might be the rapture."

"Don't be ridiculous," Jonathan shot back.

"I'm sure it's not some tale out of a book. How else do you explain this then?" asked Alex.

"Who knows? But there has to be some reason besides some book and what was written in it," replied Bobby.

"Let's get out of here," said Alex.

The friends checked out of the hotel after a couple of days. They got in the car and started to drive back over the Golden Gate Bridge. As they were coming off the bridge, they heard a sound that sounded like a trumpet. They looked around.

"Is that fire falling from the sky?" Alex asked.

Hitting the car, they saw it was hail mixed with blood and fire. They saw trees catch fire and plants burning. The drove to the nearest place to take shelter. They realized that some of the fiery hail had landed on their clothes, which started to burn. They went inside a parking garage. They started to feel pain.

"Are you sure this is something from out of a book?" asked Alex.

"Ok, so I can't explain this," said Jonathan.

"Here look," replied Alex. He held up his phone to show a passage from Revelation 8: **7,** **"**The first angel sounded, and there followed hail and fire mingled with blood, and they were cast upon the earth: and the third part of trees was burnt up, and all green grass was burnt up."

"I don't know. If I knew I would tell you. Listen this is all new to me. I don't know if you've ever seen this before, but I obviously haven't. So if you have, then let me know, otherwise get off my case. Do you think this is easy for me or anyone else? Listen, just because you come from a religious family, I don't. Is that ok with you?" Jonathan replied coldly.

"Let's not start arguing and fighting amongst each other," said Bobby.

"I'm not arguing or fighting with him, Bobby. Alex just expects us to take this at face value. This is not normal. I know what the bible said because he showed me, but it's not like I can get used to this just like that. Can you get used to this Bobby? I'm sure you've gotten used to this, huh Alex, since you seem to be reading the bible like a map to our lives being destroyed," Jonathan huffed.

"It's not like that," explained Alex. "I just know I've heard about Revelation. I've only read snippets of the book. I'm just trying to explain things, that's all."

"I'm sorry I snapped ok," said Jonathan. "Just don't force me to believe anything. I'm still processing this."

"I'm sorry too," Alex replied.

"Let's just travel the world, if in fact these are our final and last days on earth," said Bobby. "Let's go see what it's like in Israel."

"Are you insane? Why there?" asked Alex.

"Because I've always wanted to go there," Bobby replied.

"This just sounds bad," said Jonathan.

"Oh come on, let's go," said Bobby

"Fine, let's go," Jonathan and Alex replied in unison.

The fiery blood hail finally stopped. The friends drove out of the parking garage and headed to the airport. They boarded a plane, and were the only ones on it, besides the pilot and the stewardesses.

"What happens if the pilot disappears?" asked Bobby.

"What the hell are you saying?" replied Jonathan. "You're the one that wanted to visit. Why didn't you think of this beforehand? You trying to kill all of us or something? You better not say anything stupid like that again."

"I'm sorry, but I didn't think of it until now."

"Well, next time you think of something stupid like that keep it to yourself, ok? No one wants to hear that."

"Will you both calm down?" said Alex. "Everything that's going on now is not normal. We need to try and keep a clear head about all of this if possible. Overreacting won't solve anything. Plus, in the bible there is no talk of ways or solutions to avoid this except if you get raptured."

They reached Israel, got off the plane, rented a car and drove to their hotel. On the way to their hotel, they heard another sound that sounded like another trumpet. Mountains were engulfed in flames and started to break and fall into the ocean. They saw ships sinking.

At the hotel, Alex turned on the TV as the news was on. It showed dead fish rising to the top of the water and water turning red like blood. People were screaming. Oceanographers came out of the water covered in what they found out later was water turned into blood.

The news station reported that doctors and oceanographers had no explanation for the phenomenon. One person interviewed said the only time something like this ever happened was in the bible. Luckily, for Jonathan and Alex, Bobby was fluent in Hebrew, he was born in Israel and moved to the United States when he was eight. Bobby, Alex and Jonathan looked out onto the balcony. They heard a third trumpet.

A bright star from the sky came flying towards the earth. A huge impact and bright flash followed. They shielded their eyes with their arms to block the bright and powerful light. They turned their heads away. They felt waves of the impact as the hotel shook and the windows rattled. The television flickered off then on. Phone and email updates inundated the news channel they were watching. Images of the flash that hit the earth flooded the screen. Reports were coming in that while the rivers, springs and freshwater sources that hadn't turned to blood after the so-called "falling star" incident, they had become poisoned, killing many within a few hours of ingestion.

People started calling the falling star Wormwood, as in the bible. An interviewee showed a bible passage on it. People were screaming and running and were on the ground praying.

"Why did you even want to come here Bobby?" asked Alex.

"I was born here and I figured it wouldn't be as crowded as some of the other places we've been to, with people disappearing and everything. Besides, I missed the beauty that is Israel. The last time I visited here was about six years ago. Plus, I figured if this is the end of the world, then I might as well spend my last days in the place I was born."

"We need to stay inside, away from all of this craziness," said Jonathan.

"Do you really think we can avoid all of what's going on in the world today?" asked Alex.

"I don't have all the answers Alex like you seem to."

"I'm just saying there is no way to escape this and I know this is scary but we just have to ride this out."

"You ride this out since you're so into the bible now. I don't want to ride anything out, I just don't want to be here with all of this going on. You're handling it pretty well, and Bobby, too. I'm sorry if I'm terrified of this, this is not something I wanted to wake up to today or ever."

"I'm just trying not to worry too much because there is nothing we can do about any of this. I'm just glad to be here. I'm just sorry this is happening all over the world, including my home, Israel," Bobby reasoned.

"I wish this would just end. I'm so sick of seeing all of this," Jonathan said tiredly.

"Let's all get some sleep. I'm exhausted," said Alex.

"I wonder if tomorrow we'll hear the next trumpet sound, or will it be in a few days?" Bobby said out loud.

Let's get out of here and hopefully won't have to see anything else crazy, but I highly doubt that," Jonathan said.

The three friends went to their separate rooms and went to bed.

The next morning, Bobby, Jonathan and Alex all met up in the lobby. No one was downstairs. They went outside and walked around a bit. They decided to go and get something to eat.. There was a sign that said "No Water" on account of the recent poisoning. They went inside and ate. Once they finished, they decided to see the sights. They drove around and saw nothing. They didn't hear any trumpet sounds either.

"Is it supposed to be over now Alex?" Bobby asked.

"No, we're supposed to hear four more trumpets."

They saw a huge line outside of the hospital, people were on the ground not moving. Alex stopped the car. They walked by the hospital and a woman came out screaming and crying. Bobby asked her what the matter was. She told Bobby that she had given her baby some water that was supposed to be purified from the lake. She said she thought she purified it enough. She gave it to her baby because her baby wasn't feeling well. She screamed having realized she killed her own baby, saying she didn't mean to. It was the hardest thing to hear, that her little baby had died. The three friends had tears in their eyes.

They heard a sound. Someone had drunk some water and had fallen dead. A gun came out of his pocket. The woman saw the gun, grabbed it, aimed it at her head, and pulled the trigger. Nothing happened. She kept pulling the trigger over and over, but nothing happened, no bullets came out or anything. The cops came and arrested her. They checked the gun and found that it was loaded. They weren't able to figure out why the bullets never went off since the safety was off.

Alex, Bobby and Jonathan were shocked when they heard the gun was fully loaded. The cops spoke to them in English. The three gave their testimonies and so did the people that were still standing in line waiting to go into the hospital.

The three were on their way back to the hotel. They stopped at a store and got some water and snacks. "Anything else, guys?" asked the cashier.

"No, that's it, thank you," replied Jonathan. The cashier rang Jonathan up, and he handed her money.

"Oh," the cashier said, "is this the only currency you have?"

"Yes, is there something wrong?"

"No, nothing is wrong, it's just that we're doing away with money," she said.

"What do you mean by 'doing away with money?'" asked Jonathan.

Bobby and Alex looked confused.

"Well, you see, we're now using chips instead of cash. Currency is deposited to your chips and the chips can be injected or placed under your skin. Some people have given up on cash and prefer to do it this way. Of course you have these religious people who claim it's the sign of the beast. The chips leave a scar that looks like the number 666. They said it's not the mark of the beast, I heard it has something to do with like six wiring and six communications and six again for something that has to do with electronics. I'm guessing you know nothing about it, but it's been all over the news here. If you want, our pharmacy in the back can do quick work of implanting the chip, it's supposed to be covered worldwide by insurance if you have it. It doesn't take long, about an hour, and the doctor makes sure you're feeling ok after. We've had it for a while, but I guess tourists haven't thought about it at all.

"No thanks I'm not having that," Alex said.

"Oh, you won't be able to get any food or anything without the chip," the cashier replied. "Plus, there's an easy way to let people know you have the chip, 666 is stamped on your hand and forehead."

They went back to the hotel and ate some food before heading to bed. The three friends lay in their beds wondering what the next day would be like. It was getting harder and harder for each one of them to fall asleep.

The next morning, they all met up and went for a drive to check out other parts of Israel. At about 2 p.m., there was a loud trumpet sound.

"What is happening now?" asked Bobby.

"Look," said Alex, "it's here in the bible under Revelation 8:12, 'And the fourth angel sounded, and the third part of the sun was smitten, and the third part of the moon, and the third part of the stars; so as the third part of them was darkened, and the day shone not for a third part of it, and the night likewise.'"

It started to get dark. Alex looked up. He saw the clouds, lightning flashed and lit up the sky. There was thunder. "What is that? No way, it can be!" exclaimed Alex.

"What are you talking about Alex?" asked Bobby, as he looked up to the sky.

"Hey guys, I thought I saw the four horsemen! Look Bobby! Look Jonathan!" said Alex.

Bobby looked up and Jonathan pulled over to the side of the road. Lightning flashed. Both thought they saw what Alex had seen, but weren't too quick to believe. "I think we're just tired," said Bobby. Bobby and Jonathan looked up again, and this time they definitely saw what Alex had seen. All three of them kept staring at the images of the four horsemen in the clouds.

The clouds seemed to be moving. The horsemen turned to face them. The clouds came fast to meet the boys. In an instant, it seemed as if the cloud formations of the four horsemen passed through them.

The three friends looked behind them and saw the horsemen vanish. They thought they heard horses whinnying, were they hearing things, or was this really happening?

CHAPTER 2

"I can't deal with all this," said Jonathan. "This is worse than any horror film I've ever seen."

"This has me terrified," agreed Alex.

They saw Bobby trembling with fear. "Hey you ok man?" Jonathan asked. Alex put his hand on Bobby's shoulder, "Hey man, are you ok? Speak to us."

"Why is all of this happening?" Bobby started to cry. "I can't believe this is happening. I don't want the world to suffer. I can't believe this is happening," Bobby was in tears. "This is too much for me. I can't sleep at night or anything." Alex and Jonathan put their arms around Bobby and hugged him. "It's ok man."

Bobby stopped crying. "I'm sorry guys, it's been a lot. Sorry I wasn't strong enough."

"Will you shut up. This isn't normal," said Jonathan.

"Yeah man, you're good. Don't worry about it. This is just what was told and now it's coming true," Alex reasoned.

Alex started driving the car. They couldn't get over the sights they saw. Waters were still blood, dead sea animals washed ashore. Everywhere they went they saw people crying and praying. Buildings had crumbled and cars were wrecked. Once back at the hotel, Jonathan said, "Maybe it's time to leave. Then again, it would probably be best if we never left and just stayed inside. I say we stay until tomorrow and leave to go back home the next day." They all agreed.

Before they went to their rooms, Bobby said, "I'm sorry again for crying, but thanks for being there for me."

"Of course, you know we got you," said Jonathan. They each went to their rooms. Jonathan laid down on his bed, "When will this madness end?" he thought. "I hope it ends soon. I can't take much more of this. I hope Bobby and Alex are doing ok."

Bobby was in his room looking out at the sky and the scenery, tears streaming down his face.

Alex was in his room. He splashed water on his face. It was hot in his room; he was sweating profusely. He went to his bed and grabbed the sheets off the bed, balled them and tucked them under his arm. He looked at his bible on his phone and threw his phone against the wall. He went downstairs and walked outside. All he kept thinking was why did he have to live through this? Why did he, Bobby and Jonathan have to go through this? He thought about his life and all the things he had done. He wondered how long this was going to last. He went outside and saw a tree. He climbed it and thought it was too much to handle. He knew what Bobby was going through with trying to be strong. He knew what Jonathan was going through. He felt bad for always quoting the bible because it didn't make things better. He didn't want to do this anymore.

He wrapped his bed sheet around one of the branches and tied it tight around one of the strongest tree limbs. He proceeded to wrap the other end around his neck.

Bobby looked out the window and saw Alex walking outside and wondered what he was up to. He saw him climb the tree and wrap the sheet around one of the tree limbs. He was shocked as he saw Alex wrap the bed sheet around his neck. He called Jonathan on his cellphone and started to run outside.

"Hello, Bobby? What are you calling me for? Is everything ok? I just fell asleep."

"Get up Jonathan!" Bobby shouted. "Alex is trying to kill himself!"

Jonathan sprung out of bed, "Are you serious?"

"Yes, I'm serious! We have to stop him!"

Bobby and Jonathan arrived outside just as Alex jumped.

Alex couldn't take this pressure anymore. He had the sheet tied around his neck very tightly. He took a deep breath and figured he would rather die than be here.

Alex jumped. The sheet tightened around his neck but somehow came loose. The limb snapped and he fell to the ground. He saw Jonathan and Bobby run to him.

"Are you crazy? Why are you trying to take your life?" asked Jonathan.

"Get away from me!" Alex exclaimed. He ran towards an oncoming car. It hit him and he flew back a few feet. The car stopped, a woman got out of the car and Bobby and Jonathan ran over to him.

"Alex!!!!!!" Jonathan and Bobby screamed. The woman called the ambulance and the cops.

The paramedics and the cops came. The cops talked to the woman, and the woman told them what happened. The paramedics checked out Alex to see if anything was broken, they said it was a miracle that he was still alive. The paramedics asked if he was ok. He said he was fine, just sore. The cops asked him what happened, was someone after him? Alex said no. He said everything mentioned in the bible was happening, he didn't want to be alive anymore.

The cops told Bobby and Jonathan to keep an eye on Alex. The cops and the paramedics left. The woman checked on Alex again before she left.

"Bro are you ok?" Jonathan asked.

"Yeah how are you feeling man?" asked Bobby.

"I feel horrible. I hate this world that we are in now with all of this craziness. I'm sorry I bombarded you guys time after time about what was in the bible. I just don't believe what I'm seeing and that what I'm reading is coming to life. I just want to go back to normal things, but things will never be normal, not the way we know it. I used to hear all the time from preachers that these are the end times and in these last and wicked days Jesus is coming back soon, so we had better get ready, and now its here."

"Come on Alex, we still have each other bro," said Jonathan. "I'm sorry that I got on your case. I never asked how you were doing," he added.

"No it's my fault. I never thought about how this could be affecting you two."

"You do know you can talk to us about anything, we're your bros," Bobby said.

"I know, and with each trumpet sound it has gotten worse. It was more horrific than what I've read. I also can't sleep at night. The thing with the four horsemen really freaked me out. Listen, all we have is each other. Let's try and help each other stay sane and make sure each other is good.

"Agreed," said Jonathan. "Alex come on, let's go."

Jonathan and Bobby made sure Alex was ok. They went for a walk and got some food while they were out walking. They wanted to keep Alex distracted so he wouldn't try to commit suicide again. They were worried about Alex. The image of him hanging from the tree and jumping in front of a car scared them and made them realize that they do have each other and any little bickering they had wasn't nearly as big as their friend trying to take his own life.

They went back to the hotel and stayed in the room with Alex to make sure that he didn't try to commit suicide or anything else that would harm him. For the next couple of days, they watched Alex very carefully. They were supposed to go back to the United States, but decided to stay in Israel and make sure he didn't try anything on the plane. Jonathan and Bobby took turns watching him at night. When the third day came, Alex apologized to Bobby and Jonathan for causing so much trouble and anxiety. Jonathan and Bobby told Alex not to worry about it and that they were glad he was just alive.

They woke up and decided to get some food before going to the airport. Jonathan and Bobby both felt like it would be a great idea to head back to the States now. They saw on the news that it was going to be a nice day. The news anchors said it seemed like everything had calmed down and that people were trying to get back to normal.

They felt the hotel tremble. Hanging flower plants started to fall, baggage carts tumbled and crashed against doors. Televisions started to fall on the floor. Thunder could be heard outside.

"It's an earthquake!" said Bobby.

The three friends found tables and desks to hide under. The earthquake lasted an hour. Car alarms went off, some people fell off their balconies and were severely injured. The earthquake finally stopped. The three friends helped clear doors of baggage carts. They checked on other people to make sure they were alright. They went outside to check if there was more damage. Some trees had fallen. They turned on the radio to find out the airport had sustained some damage, that some of the ceiling had collapsed and that it was a complete mess. Flights back to the States were canceled. The three went back inside and asked if they could extend their stay. They were able to.

They went to the car to see the extent of damage. They drove further out than where they were. More trees had fallen. They came to a clearing and saw a bright light in the sky. It looked as if it were a person. The person turned out to be an angel.

The angel said in a loud voice, "Woe, woe, woe, to the inhabitants of the earth, by reason of the trumpet of the three other angels, which are yet to sound!"

Alex looked at his phone and said, "Guys look, this is the angel warning us, and the fifth trumpet is about to sound." The angel departed and the friends heard the trumpet sound.

Alex glanced at his phone, which was still recording. There was something falling down from the sky, it hit the ground. The ground shook. There arose a dark figure dressed in a black robe and hood. The figure lifted up its hand.

"Guys we need to hurry and get out of here!" Alex showed them a passage from Revelation 9:1-11,

"1   And the fifth angel sounded, and I saw a star fall from heaven unto the earth: and to him was given the key of the bottomless pit.

"2   And he opened the bottomless pit; and there arose a smoke out of the pit, as the smoke of a great furnace; and the sun and the air were darkened by reason of the smoke of the pit.

"3   And there came out of the smoke locusts upon the earth: and unto them was given power, as the scorpions of the earth have power.

"4   And it was commanded them that they should not hurt the grass of the earth, neither any green thing, neither any tree; but only those men which have not the seal of God in their foreheads.

"5   And to them it was given that they should not kill them, but that they should be tormented five months: and their torment was as the torment of a scorpion, when he striketh a man.

"6   And in those days shall men seek death, and shall not find it; and shall desire to die, and death shall flee from them.

"7   And the shapes of the locusts were like unto horses prepared unto battle; and on their heads were as it were crowns like gold, and their faces were as the faces of men.

"8   And they had hair as the hair of women, and their teeth were as the teeth of lions.

"9   And they had breastplates, as it were breastplates of iron; and the sound of their wings was as the sound of chariots of many horses running to battle.

"10 And they had tails like unto scorpions, and there were stings in their tails: and their power was to hurt men five months.

"11 And they had a king over them, which is the angel of the bottomless pit, whose name in the Hebrew tongue is Abaddon, but in the Greek tongue hath his name Apollyon."

They hurried back to the car. Jonathan and Bobby looked back, the figure stuck the key into the ground. The sky became dark. Smoke came out of the ground and the locusts that were described in the bible came out of the hole. The figure raised its hand and stretched its hand out as if pointing towards the friends. Alex slammed his foot on the gas and was driving as fast as he could.

Thunder could be heard and lightning flashed throughout the sky. He drove around slow cars. In the rearview mirror it seemed like the locusts were following them. He kept speeding. Once at

Armageddon

the hotel, the three friends scrambled out of the car and ran to Jonathan's room and locked the door behind them.

Jonathan looked through the window. "Guys you're not going to believe this, but look at all of these locusts." Alex and Bobby peered for themselves.

The bible said one could not see anything but locusts for miles. They slammed against the window.

The window started to crack. The three friends gasped and backed away. Jonathan fell on the bed, Bobby tripped and fell over a chair, Alex backed into a table. Alex helped Bobby and Jonathan up. Alex opened the door of the room, and as soon as he did so, the window broke and the locusts flew inside. The friends ran to the elevator and pushed the call button frantically. It took awhile for the elevator to arrive. The friends heard a sound and saw locusts coming out of the room. They ran down the stairs and heard screaming in the hallways. People ran into the stairwell, screaming in pain as they were stung by locusts. The boys started to panic, they descended the steps two or three at a time, until they reached the main floor. They ran towards the entrance. They saw the hotel staff swatting locusts, trying to hit them with papers, magazines and chairs. They screamed in pain as they were stung. The boys rushed out and hurried into their car. Jonathan slammed on the gas while in reverse. As they were leaving, they saw all of the hotel guests coming out in one massive group followed by locusts. It was almost like a scene from a zombie movie. Jonathan floored it out of the parking lot. The locusts flew low in front of cars, blocking drivers' view.

Cars swerved in and out of lanes, crashing into trees, buildings, other cars, and even hitting people. Jonathan drove fast, swerving out of the way of oncoming cars heading directly at him. He eventually went off the road to avoid crashing into wild drivers. The locusts were hitting car windows with full force until they finally broke, all anyone could hear were screams. The locusts finally broke their own car windows and stung Jonathan and Bobby. They screamed in pain.

"Pull over. I'll drive," said Alex.

"I got it. Soon as we get to a spot, I'll stop and you can take over. I can manage a little pain." Jonathan kept driving. The pain kept increasing. He was in so much pain that he was swerving all over the road. Alex grabbed the wheel and was trying to get the car on the road.

"I got it," repeated Jonathan.

"Pull over. I'll drive you and Bobby. Looks like you're in a tremendous amount of pain."

"I got it, thanks, but I can manage it." said Jonathan.

Alex sat back. As soon as he did, Jonathan crashed into the side of a hill. "Is everyone alright?" asked Alex.

"I'm in severe pain from where I got stung by those weird looking locusts. Other than that, just shaken up by the crash," replied Bobby.

Alex looked at Jonathan, who had a bloody nose. He shook Jonathan. "Hey Jon, you ok? Jonathan answer me! You good?"

Jonathan started to move. "I feel like I've been hit by a truck, I'm in so much pain right now from those locusts."

"How are you feeling Alex?" asked Bobby. "Did you get stung?"

"No, I didn't," replied Alex.

"How long is this supposed to last?", asked Jonathan.

"The bible says the torment is supposed to last for five months. That's a hell of a long time to endure this kind of pain and everything. We better get to higher ground and make sure we're ok. Can you all make it?" asked Alex.

"Yeah, we can make it. Oh God, my body feels weird," said Bobby.

"What do you mean feels weird?" asked Alex.

"Well I didn't want to tell you, but I went and got that chip injected into me. I knew you were going to go on about the whole religious thing, and now it seems like you're right about everything," said Bobby.

"Why would you do that?" Alex continued, "It says in Revelation 13:16-18 '**16** And he caused all, both small and great, rich and poor, free and bond, to receive a mark in their right hand, or in their foreheads:

'17 And that no man might buy or sell, save he that had the mark, or the name of the beast, or the number of his name.

'18 Here is wisdom. Let him that hath understanding count the number of the beast: for it is the number of a man; and his number is six hundred threescore and six.'"

"Because I need to eat and drink and I do not regret it," replied Bobby. "Listen, I didn't believe you at first about all of this nonsense and it seemed as if you and the bible were telling the truth, but I need food and drink, all humans need food. I'm not a religious person and this scared me to death, but we will have to eat food sometime and I'm not going to go on faith to feed me."

CHAPTER 3

Alex, Bobby and Jonathan headed to the Hill of Megiddo. When they finally made it to the top, Alex looked around. "Well, we can rest here for a little. There are some locusts still here, not as much as before."

Jonathan and Bobby were drinking water and taking some medicine for the pain they were feeling from the stings. They ate some chips and some sandwiches they had saved from the night before at the hotel. Alex seemed to be staring out in the distance. They called him, but Alex didn't reply. They tried again and threw little pebbles at him to get his attention. Still, Alex didn't move or say a word. They walked over to him; they saw his hands trembling and saw the look of fear on his face.

"Hey bro, what's the matter?" asked Bobby.

"Hey you good Alex?" added Jonathan.

"We have to leave. We need to leave right now. We can't be here; this is not good we need to leave," Alex said over and over.

"Where do you expect us to go and how? The car is totaled."

"We need to hitchhike. We can't stay here; we have to leave right now. We will die if we stay here."

"What are you going on about?" asked Jonathan.

"This is Tel Megiddo, otherwise known as the Hill of Megiddo. This is the site where the battle of Armageddon is supposed to take place. This is where the Anti-Christ and his followers and Jesus and His army are supposed to fight. We will die here. If we get caught up in this battle, millions of people will die, including us. We need to find a way to stay out of it come battle time. Let's look around and see where we can hide unharmed until this battle blows over. Let's split up and see what we can find, make sure your phones are on. If we find anything, we can call or text each other."

Everyone split up. They searched high and low. No one was having any luck at all. Jonathan thought he found a place to hide but he was mistaken. Bobby searched high and low, but he could not find anything either. They all gathered back without any luck.

"Does the bible say where they'll be coming from in case we're still here?" asked Jonathan.

"No, the bible doesn't say anything like that," replied Alex. There was a loud sound. It was the sixth trumpet. "Oh no, this is not good."

"What is it now?" asked Bobby.

"Here, in Revelation 9:13-21-.

'13 And the sixth angel sounded, and I heard a voice from the four horns of the golden altar which is before God,

'14 Saying to the sixth angel which had the trumpet, Loose the four angels which are bound in the great river Euphrates.

'15 And the four angels were loosed, which were prepared for an hour, and a day, and a month, and a year, for to slay the third part of men.

'16 And the number of the army of the horsemen were two hundred thousand thousand: and I heard the number of them.

'17 And thus I saw the horses in the vision, and them that sat on them, having breastplates of fire, and of jacinth, and brimstone: and the heads of the horses were as the heads of lions; and out of their mouths issued fire and smoke and brimstone.

'18 By these three was the third part of men killed, by the fire, and by the smoke, and by the brimstone, which issued out of their mouths.

'19 For their power is in their mouth, and in their tails: for their tails were like unto serpents, and had heads, and with them they do hurt.

'20 And the rest of the men which were not killed by these plagues yet repented not of the works of their hands, that they should not worship devils, and idols of gold, and silver, and brass, and stone, and of wood: which neither can see, nor hear, nor walk:

'21 Neither repented they of their murders, nor of their sorceries, nor of their fornication, nor of their thefts.'"

Bobby, Alex, and Jonathan heard the horses and saw the horsemen and the army go forth throughout the world. The thunder had sounded even louder than before, there was lightning flashing across the sky as they appeared. The three friends thought it would have stopped, but it didn't. The lightning and thunder kept sounding and flashing and a huge thick fog arose.

"Do you hear something?" asked Alex.

"No I… Wait, I do hear something now," replied Jonathan. "I hear what sounds like singing and what happened at the church we went to that had praise and worship. I hear someone saying, 'Oh holy God we worship You.'"

"I hear something too," replied Bobby. "I hear something that sounds like chanting."

The fog started to lift. Alex, Bobby and Jonathan saw what seemed like two huge armies, one side was praising God and the other side was cursing God. On one side were prophets, pastors, evangelists, apostles, people that were anointed by God. On the other side were the anti-Christs, false prophets, warlocks, voodoo priests, seers, witches, psychics, root workers and Satanists. Above each in the sky there were angels on one side and demons on the other. Alex realized they were in the middle of the two sides. He told Bobby and Jonathan to run. "We need to get out of the way. Sorry everyone, we are not involved in this." Alex, Bobby and Jonathan kept running straight ahead, hoping to get out the way of both sides. As they ran, more and more warriors kept appearing on both sides, on the ground and sky as well. The fighting started. Both sides rushed into battle, separating Bobby, Alex and Jonathan. Alex looked back and saw that both sides were fighting. He didn't see Bobby or Jonathan, he called out to them, but never got an answer. He went looking all over for them. He must've spent about two hours. Their phones rang but went to voicemail.

Jonathan found his way out. He called for Alex and Bobby, but he didn't receive a reply as well. He saw that he had missed a few calls from Alex. He called Alex and Alex picked up but Alex couldn't explain where he was. They said they would both try to find each other. Neither one had seen Bobby. Bobby made his way out but wasn't able to see Jonathan or Alex.

After about three hours, Alex finally found Jonathan. "I found you, so glad you're ok."

"Yeah thanks," replied Jonathan. "So I'm guessing you haven't found Bobby yet have you?"

"No, I haven't seen him since before we tried to get away from the fighting."

"Let's hurry and see if we can find him."

The fighting stopped; the battle of Armageddon had only lasted a day. There were bodies everywhere, millions of dead bodies. Alex saw someone moving. It was Bobby. Jonathan ran over to Bobby and hugged him. Bobby had found his way back to the top of Megiddo. He was out of breath. "I'm so glad to see you guys. There were bodies everywhere no matter where I turned or where I ran to. There was fighting everywhere. It was so scary," said Bobby. "Same here," Alex and Jonathan said in unison.

They decided to walk back down to where the car was and there was a river of blood flowing, literally up to a horse's bridle, just as it said in the bible. When Jonathan, Alex and Bobby tried to get to the car, blood came up to their chests, they had to turn back and make their way to the top of the hill.

When they made it back, Bobby fell to the ground. Alex and Jonathan tried to help him up, but they noticed his shirt was bulging and from underneath spilled out his intestines. "I was injured in the battle trying to find my way out. I guess this is what happens when you get the mark of the beast, huh Alex?"

"Bobby I don't know what happens. I'm so sorry about this," replied Alex.

"It wasn't your fault, I got the mark of the beast on my own, no one forced me."

Out of nowhere, an angel appeared in the sky and said, "All fowls that fly in the midst of heaven come and gather yourselves unto the supper of the great God." The birds and beasts came to Tel Megiddo.

"Oh no this is not good," said Alex.

"Why not?" asked Jonathan.

Look at what the bible says in Revelation 19:17-21-

'17 And I saw an angel standing in the sun; and he cried with a loud voice, saying to all the fowls that fly in the midst of heaven, Come and gather yourselves together unto the supper of the great God;

'18 That ye may eat the flesh of kings, and the flesh of captains, and the flesh of mighty men, and the flesh of horses, and of them that sit on them, and the flesh of all men, both free and bond, both small and great.

'19 And I saw the beast, and the kings of the earth, and their armies, gathered together to make war against him that sat on the horse, and against his army.

'20 And the beast was taken, and with him the false prophet that wrought miracles before him, with which he deceived them that had received the mark of the beast, and them that worshipped his image. These both were cast alive into a lake of fire burning with brimstone.

'21 And the remnant was slain with the sword of him that sat upon the horse, which sword proceeded out of his mouth: and all the fowls were filled with their flesh.'"

The birds and the beasts started to eat the dead bodies. A bird swooped down and started to eat Bobby's intestines. Bobby screamed. Alex and Jonathan tried to help him, but the beast of the lands stood between Alex and Jonathan. Bobby died a few seconds later, his body eaten by the birds and the beasts of the land.

Jonathan and Alex were crying and screaming. They started to walk back in the direction of the hotel. They came to where the blood wasn't as high. A car picked them up. The couple in it asked if they were alright. New over the car radio reported that flights were leaving out of the airport to go back to the United States.

They checked out of the hotel and made their way back to the airport. They got on a plane and landed back in the United States.

They hadn't said a word since being on the plane. Jonathan started to cry. Alex told him it's ok, then Alex started to cry. They heard a loud trumpet and saw a figure in the sky. Alex explained this was the time when Jesus would appear and come to reign. Jonathan repented for his sins.

That day onward Jonathan and Alex worshipped God and thanked Him for saving them, that they didn't die during Armageddon. God told them that He was going to make a new heaven and a new earth.

The old earth and the old heaven were wiped out and a new earth and a new heaven was created according to the bible.

www.ingramcontent.com/pod-product-compliance
Lightning Source LLC
LaVergne TN
LVHW020447080526
838202LV00055B/5364